TOO MANY DOGS

Jeff Gottesfeld

SADDLEBACK
EDUCATIONAL PUBLISHING

red rhino b**oo**ks™

With more titles on the way …

SADDLEBACK
EDUCATIONAL PUBLISHING
www.sdlback.com

ISBN-13: 978-1-62250-951-5
ISBN-10: 1-62250-951-X
eBook: 978-1-63078-174-3

Printed in Guangzhou, China
NOR/0215/CA21500098

19 18 17 16 15   1 2 3 4 5

Eva

Age: 12

Least Favorite Chore: dusting shelves

Career Goal: to run a charity that feeds hungry kids

Favorite Music: modern Hawaiian hip-hop

Best Quality: level-headed

CHARACTERS

carmen

Age: 11½

Greatest Fear: being alone outside after dark

Special Talent: can say hello in twenty-eight different languages

Favorite School Subject: geography

Best Quality: cooperative

1
MONEY!

Eva White pushed her curly dark hair off her forehead. Then she looked up at her mom. "Can I have ten dollars?"

"Ten bucks?" Mrs. White frowned. "That's a lot of money. What do you need ten dollars for?"

Things $10 can buy

Eva's best friend, Carmen Flores, spoke up. Her voice was soft. "Stuff. It costs a lot to be a teen these days."

The summer sun was hot and bright. Mrs. White moved to the kitchen window to pull down the shade. Then she laughed.

← Too hot!

"That's funny. You guys aren't teens. You're in sixth grade. Anyway, you two know the drill. Your mom and I have a deal, Carmen. If you guys want to go to the movies, we pay. If you need shoes, we pay. Books, we pay. Cell phones, we pay. You know, when I was your age—"

Eva held up a hand. "Mom? And I'm sorry to cut in like this."

"Yes?"

"When you say, 'When I was your age?' That was a *really* long time ago."

Everyone cracked up. Even Mrs. White.

The girls' moms and dads were best friends too. Just like Eva and Carmen. The adults agreed on everything. They loved to cook. They loved to go to plays. And all four hated pets.

There were no pets in their homes. Not even a goldfish. It was too bad for Eva and Carmen. Each girl wanted a pet. But it was a total no go.

NEEDS A HOME

"Look, Mom," Eva went on. "It's just to go to Chill. With our buds."

Meet us at
Chill

Chill was the local frozen yogurt place. Their friends met up there at four o'clock most days. Eva and Carmen wanted to go too. But Mrs. Flores and Mrs. White said Chill was a waste of money.

Mrs. White looked away for a moment. Then she turned back to the girls. "Okay. I get it. But I think if you want spending money, you need to find a way to earn it."

Eva sighed. Her mom did not get it. There were few jobs kids could get these days. No one her age cut lawns or even babysat. There were high school kids happy to do that.

"We don't know what to do," Eva said.

"Figure it out," Mrs. White said. "Here." She dug into her jeans for a twenty dollar bill. Then she put it on the kitchen table. "If you can earn twenty dollars, I'll match it."

She left the room. The cash stayed on the table.

Carmen winked at Eva. "I say we grab it and go to Chill."

Eva shook her head. "Nope. I want us to earn it. And I think I know how."

What's better?

OR

2
SCRUB IT

The two girls went to the Wongs' house. A dirty camper was parked in the driveway. They stepped up to the door of the big house. They carried buckets. Sponges. And soap.

"Richie Wong told me they're going to the beach for a week," Eva told Carmen. "Do you think they want to tow a dirty camper?"

We can do this!

Carmen pointed a finger at Eva. "Hold on. Can't they just go to a car wash?"

Eva smiled. "Nope. Campers can't fit. So, we doing this or not?"

"We're doing it." Carmen pushed the doorbell.

Mr. Wong opened the door.

Eva had planned what to say.

"Hi, Mister Wong. I'm Eva White. This is my bud Carmen. We know your son Richie from school. He said you're going to the beach. We want to wash your camper for the trip. We're cheap. Fifteen dollars. Come on. You don't want to tow a dirty camper to the shore. Right?"

NOT beach-ready

Mr. Wong peered at the girls. "No. I sure don't. Which is why I'll tell Richie to do it."

Oops. Eva felt dumb. She had not thought of that. But they had walked all the way over here …

She gave Mr. Wong a big smile. "Well … we'd need Richie's help. It's a big job."

"We were just going to say that," Carmen added. "We would share the money."

"Too bad you won't do it without Richie," Mr. Wong said. "He's out shopping with his mom."

"Oh," Carmen said.

"Wait," Eva added. "We don't need Richie's help. We can do it on our own."

"If you do it for ten bucks, it's a deal," Mr. Wong said.

Eva put out her hand. "Deal."

Mr. Wong shook it. Then he said he'd get the girls a ladder.

Now it's official

The camper was huge. Three hours later, the girls were still scrubbing. Mr. Wong held the ladder so the girls could get up to the camper roof.

"How come it's so dusty?" Eva asked.

She was hot. She was sweaty. They had a lot more to do.

"Painted Desert. Arizona. Good times," Mr. Wong said. He got himself a cold drink. "Keep at it, girls."

It feels like the desert here!

No drinks for us?!

It took five hours to wash the camper. Mr. Wong paid them. Eva did some mental math. "Two girls. Five hours. That's a total of ten hours. Ten bucks. A dollar an hour!"

Carmen moaned.

"Well, it's more like two an hour," Eva said. She got the buckets. "My mom will put in ten more."

"Yeah. Once," Carmen muttered sadly.

They heard a dog yapping down the street.

"That dog sounds like *it* just washed a camper," Eva said.

The dog howled even louder. Eva got worried. There was just something about the sound.

She put down the buckets. "Wait for me."

She ran to the sound of the dog. It was in a backyard at the end of the block. Eva peered through a fence. It was an old beagle. When it saw Eva, it trotted over to her.

The little guy making the BIG noise

"Hi there," Eva told the dog.

"Girl! Who are you? And why are you on my land?"

Uh-oh.

Someone had yelled at her. And that someone did not sound happy.

3
SWAPS

Eva turned. Right behind her was a mean-looking old man. He had angry eyes. He held two canes. He was short and round. If he fell over, he might roll down the street. He took two steps toward Eva.

"What are you doing on my land?" The old man banged one cane on the walk.

"I'm ... I'm ... I'm Eva White. I was just

walking by. I heard your dog. I figured maybe it was sick. Really. That's all."

"She's telling the truth!"

Carmen came running up. That was good. Eva was not alone with this crazy old man.

"What do you know about this?" the man asked her.

"My name is Carmen. It's just what Eva said." Carmen stayed calm. "We just washed the Wongs' camper. We heard the dog. Eva was afraid it was sick. That's all."

The man nodded. "I see."

"So?" Carmen asked.

"So what?"

"So. Is your dog sick?"

"Of course the dog is sick. An okay dog doesn't howl like that! And it's my fault," the man said. "I don't take care of him the way I should. He has a name, you know. Swaps."

"Swaps? Like a swap meet?" Eva asked. What a strange name for a dog.

The man shook his head. "Don't you kids know anything? When I was your age, there was a horse named Swaps. A champ. I loved that racehorse."

There was that phrase again. "When I was your age." Eva wondered if every adult used it.

Swaps howled again. It was so sad. Why would this man not take care of his dog? It made Eva want to take Swaps home. But no way would her mom and dad let her. Same thing for Carmen's parents. But still.

Anyway, it was time to go. This old guy gave her the creeps.

"Well," Eva said. "I guess we'll be—"

The old man cleared his throat. "You girls washed the Wongs' camper?"

Carmen nodded. "That's right."

"To earn money," Eva added. "Um, we've got to go now."

He cleared his throat again. "Maybe you girls could cure Swaps. That is, if you want to make more money."

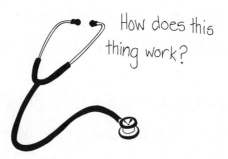

How does this thing work?

Eva shook her head. She was no dog doctor. He needed a vet, not a sixth grader. "No thank you, Mister ... whatever your name is."

"Mister Gold," the old man said. "Bill Gold. And I know what you think. You think I'm a loon who needs to take his dog to the vet. But I'm telling you. You girls could cure him."

Eva had to ask. "How?"

"Walk him. Three times a day. Half an hour in the morning. Forty-five minutes in the afternoon. Half an hour at sunset. I'll pay ten bucks a walk. Cash. "

We could do that!

Mr. Gold shook his finger at the girls. "I can't walk him anymore. Not with these pegs I got. All this dog wants to do is get out. What do you say? Don't say yes and then not show up."

Eva did more mental math. Ten dollars a walk was thirty dollars a day! For less than two hours of work. Walking a dog.

Her head reeled. If they did it, they would not just have money for Chill. They'd have money for anything they wanted.

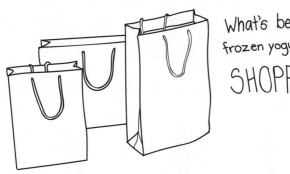

What's better than frozen yogurt? SHOPPING!

4
KA-CHING!

"Go, Swaps, go!"

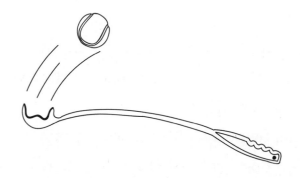

Eva flung the ball to the edge of the dog park. Swaps tore after it. For two days now, she and Carmen had walked the beagle. This was the first time they took him to the dog park. He could be off leash there. The park was full of dogs. Big dogs. Little dogs. Fat dogs. Thin dogs. Cute dogs. Ugly dogs. All the dogs were glad to be free and running.

Eva and Carmen were as happy as any dog there. This was as close as they would come to real life with a pet.

"Go, Swaps! Go!" Eva cried again.

The dog grabbed the ball. Then he tore back to Eva. He dropped the ball at her feet and panted.

"More?" Eva asked.

Swaps barked three times.

"Okay! Go!" Eva flung the ball again. Off went Swaps. As the dog ran, Eva looked for

Carmen. There she was. She was talking with a man and a woman. The couple had a brown dog. A mutt.

Eva reached into her pocket. Inside was a card. She and Carmen had made a bunch of them.

❀ DOG WALKING & PET SITTING ❀

LOTS OF LOVE FOR YOUR DOG

LOW PRICES

CALL EVA OR CARMEN

The card had a phone number and email. Even if they only had Swaps, the girls would make good money. If they got more dogs? They could buy Chill for all their buds.

Eva threw the ball six more times. When Swaps came back the final time, Carmen did too. The dog sat at their feet to rest.

"How'd you do?" Eva asked.

Carmen rubbed her hands together. "How much time do we have?"

"What do you mean?" asked Eva.

"I mean, how would you like to make more money? A lot more."

Carmen handed Eva a sheet of paper. On the paper were five names. And five phone numbers. "Our cards worked! We have more dogs to walk. A lot more! We're going to be rich."

Eva was thrilled. She dropped to her knees and took Swaps by the front paws. "I hope you like walking with other dogs."

Swaps barked. He seemed to like the idea. At least that's what Eva hoped.

5
CHILL

Eva and Carmen were the first to get to Chill. Their buds would be there soon. Chill worked like this: There were soft-serve yogurt pumps. A kid filled a cup with the flavors they wanted.

There were all kinds of toppings. You chose whatever looked good. And you'd get as much as you wanted. The price was by weight. There was a scale at the register.

Carmen likes fruit and a little granola

Eva likes candy and A LOT of sprinkles

The girls had already made a plan. They went to the owner, Mrs. Peters. If Chill was open, Mrs. Peters was there.

"Hi, girls," Mrs. Peters said. "Where are your cups?"

Eva took forty dollars from her pocket. Carmen did the same. They handed the money to Mrs. Peters.

The owner looked at the money. "Um, girls? You pay *after* you get your yogurt. Not before."

"That's not for us. It's for our friends," Eva told her.

"We want to pay for everyone," Carmen added.

Mrs. Peters wore a blue Chill cap. She pushed the brim up. "There's eighty dollars here. Did you girls win the lottery?"

Eva shook her head. "Nope. We're working."

"And you're buying yogurt for your friends?" Mrs. Peters was amazed. "You are really nice. Or nuts. Or both." She put the money in the register. "Okay. Eighty dollars. I'll keep track. Then I'll tell you when it's all spent. You're going have some happy friends."

Paul Crutcher and Max Allen were the first kids to show up. Paul was the class clown. Max was his bestie. They got their cups, filled them, and went to pay. Mrs. Peters told them it was paid for.

"Really?" Paul asked.

"Really. Go thank Carmen and Eva," she told the boys.

The boys hustled over to the girls.

"You paid for us?" Paul asked. "But why?"

"Just being nice," Eva said.

"We've got jobs," Carmen told him.

"So we've got money," Eva added.

More kids they knew came into the shop. Paul called to them. "Hey! Carmen and Eva are buying! Eat a lot!"

The other kids shouted with joy. Paul sat down with Eva and Carmen. He was a short boy who wore baggy shorts. "So. What's the deal? Where do you guys work? *Here?*"

Are those pants or shorts?

"Nope. We're dog walkers." Eva said it proudly.

Paul was about to eat some yogurt. He put down his spoon. "You mean people pay you to walk their dogs?"

Carmen nodded. "Ten dollars a walk. It's so easy."

"We make a *lot* of money," Eva shared.

"What we paid for the yogurt? We can make it back in one day."

Paul rubbed his chin. "How long have you been doing this? How did you find the dogs?"

Eva told him the whole story. She even showed him one of their cards.

Paul took it. "You guys are smart. Can I keep this?"

"Sure!" Eva said. "And if you ever need a dog walked? Give us a call."

6
POOPED

A week later, Eva was pooped.

There was Swaps's poop. A chow's poop. Worst of all, the poop from a Great Dane named Dee Dee. Dee Dee was female. She was as gentle as a kitten. But twice as big as Eva.

Dee Dee likes to give hugs

The girls took plastic bags on all dog walks. For walks with Dee Dee, Eva needed extra-big bags.

Carmen was pooped too. She did not have any Great Danes. But she did have three dogs to walk. Three times a day.

That's a lot of...

The money rolled in. For three dogs, Eva made thirty dollars a walk. That was ninety dollars a day. Each walk took an hour. She was amazed how many people would pay to get their dog walked.

Eva knew she would never have a dog. But if she did have a dog, she would walk it herself. The dogs got so excited when she came to get them. It was the best part of their day. To have a dog and not walk it yourself just seemed dumb.

Ready for my walk!

She was out with the dogs when a text came from Carmen.

"How u doing?"

Eva texted back. "K. Hey! I have idea."

"??" Carmen texted.

Eva looked at Dee Dee. She was *so* big. But she was also a wimp. Other dogs made her shake with fear. Even little ones. At first, it was funny. Then it stopped being funny. A scared Great Dane was hard to walk.

"Can we get extra $ for big dogs?"

Carmen texted right back. "Define big."

Eva's thumbs flew on her phone. "Dee Dee is BIG!!!!"

But she had to stop texting. Swaps and the chow started barking and pulling. Dee Dee tried to hide behind Eva. Then Eva saw why. Down the street was someone else with dogs. Three of them. They were barking too. Uh-oh. The last thing she wanted was a dog fight.

Everything was fine, until...

Eva moved her dogs off the sidewalk. She would walk them in the street. The other dogs came closer. Her dogs—not Dee Dee—tried to get to them. The barking got louder. She ordered, "Stop it!"

Then Eva saw who was walking the other dogs. It was a kid. In fact, she knew him.

Paul Crutcher.

Paul Crutcher? What was he doing with three dogs? Eva got a sick feeling. She had told Paul all about the business. Had he …

"Hi, Eva!" Paul said. "Thanks for all the info. Looks like you've got competition."

"You're walking dogs for money?" Eva asked.

"Yup! I'm making as much money as you. More, even. Max is helping too."

Eva was so mad. "You stole our idea!"

Paul grinned. "Hey. That's life. If you ever need a dog walked? Call me. Here's my card."

He flipped a card toward Eva. She picked it up as he headed away. She almost tore it up. Instead, she jammed it in a pocket. Okay. Paul wanted to take her on? Let the best walker win.

Paul & Max
The **BEST** dog walkers around!

← This means WAR!

7
SPOILED

It was two days later. Eva and Carmen waited by the front door. They had gotten the call the night before. The client was named Ms. Wax. She said she had to go away for three days. There had been no time to plan.

Ms. Wax had a great little dog. It needed care. There was no one else who could do it. Could the girls walk her? And feed her too? She would give them the key to her house.

Eva and Carmen talked it over. Their parents called Ms. Wax. She worked for the post office. She had great references. The moms left it up to the girls. It was okay if the girls wanted to take on this job. But they had to be sure it would work with the other dogs.

Then Ms. Wax called again. She said the girls were her very last hope. She said she could pay forty dollars a day.

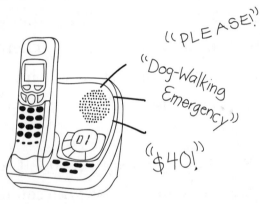

"PLEASE!"

"Dog-Walking Emergency"

"$40!"

That sealed it. Carmen had three dogs to walk. Eva only had two. Swaps and the Great Dane. The chow's family was on vacation. So Eva would take on the new dog. They would share the money.

The front door opened. Ms. Wax came out. A small white dog followed her. The dog was a mutt. She had a sweet face and a big belly. She came to each girl. Eva petted her head. The dog seemed nice. She even rolled over to show Eva her belly. Eva petted her there. The dog grunted happily.

Meet Maggie

"Her name is Maggie," Ms. Wax said. "She is a poodle-schnauzer mix. I call her a schnoodle. Don't worry. She isn't due until I come back."

Eva's eyes got big.

"Due?" she asked. "As in puppies? You didn't say anything about puppies."

Due?! Puppies?! No way!

"I didn't? Oh, I'm so sorry. I've been so crazy. Planning this trip and all," Ms. Wax said. She had a notebook in her right hand. "It's so last minute. Anyway, it is no big thing. I'll be back well before then. Here. Read this. I only have one. You'll have to share. It has all of Maggie's rules."

Eva took the notebook. It said what to do with Maggie. Where to walk her. When to walk her. How to mix her food. How to play with her. Even how she liked her water. She liked one ice cube in her bowl. Not two. One.

How To Take Care of Maggie

seriously?!

Eva thought it was a bit much. The food was fine. But an ice cube? And where to take her for a walk? That was nuts. There were other dogs she had to walk. It was a team thing.

"Ms. Wax? Is it okay if I walk her where I want?" Eva asked.

"You can try. But you may not have much luck. How about you do your first walk now? I'll get her leash."

Ms. Wax went inside. Maggie followed.

"What do you think?" Eva asked Carmen.

Carmen grinned. "I think it's forty bucks a day. I'd bake her pizza and walk her to New York for that kind of money."

Carmen makes a <u>mean</u> pizza

Eva looked at the notebook again. She read the food section.

Maggie likes her dry food soaked in warm water. Warm. Not hot. Warm. If you put your finger in and have to take it out, that's too hot. Throw it out and start again.

Eva shook her head. This was silly. Why not just put it in the fridge for a half hour?

Ms. Wax came back with Maggie on the leash. "Who wants to take her?"

"We'll both take her," Eva said. "Okay, Carmen?"

"Sure!"

Ms. Wax went inside. Eva led Maggie to the street. To the left was the route Ms. Wax had set out. To the right was where they would pick up the Great Dane.

Eva tried to take Maggie to the right. The dog would not go. She pulled left. Eva tugged her to the right. The dog tugged left. Then the dog sat down. When Eva tried to coax her, Maggie did not move. In fact, she cried.

Ms. Wax came outside. "What are you girls doing?"

Eva flushed. "We're walking Maggie. She wants to go a certain way."

"Then take her that way. That's what I'm paying you for."

Ms. Wax went back inside.

The girls looked at each other. Carmen rolled her eyes. Maggie might be cute. But she was also a spoiled brat.

Princess Maggie

(Yes, that's really her bed.)

8
RUNAWAY!

The next day was a mess. Rain came down in sheets. The wind howled. Almost no cars were on the street. The TV said it was a bad summer storm. It would be like this until sunset. There was flooding in many places.

Eva still had to walk the dogs. So did

Carmen. Carmen had stayed over with Eva. In the morning, Mrs. Flores had come over too. She was visiting with Mrs. White.

When they saw the rain, they begged their moms for help.

"Please? Please?" Carmen begged. "Please help us walk the dogs!"

Carmen's mom shook her head. "Nope."

"But it's pouring!" Carmen said.

"You'll wear boots. Do your jobs," Mrs. Flores said. "I don't want to hear any more."

Ready for the rain

"That's why they call it work," said Eva's mother. "It isn't always fun. When I was your age, I had to shovel snow."

"Mom?" Eva asked.

"Yeah?"

"Not helpful."

That was that. They would get no help. Their moms would not even drop them off. Eva and Carmen put on boots and slickers. But by the time Eva walked to get Swaps, she was soaked. Swaps seemed to love the rain. So did Dee Dee.

The next stop was Maggie. It took ten wet minutes to walk there.

Eva had a key to the house. She stepped inside and called.

"Come on, Maggie! Walkie time!"

Maggie ran to her. She let Eva leash her up. But with the first step into the rain, she stopped. Then she barked over and over.

"Come on, girl," Eva said. She had the other dogs too. They had to get moving. "Don't be spoiled, Maggie. You have to walk. If you go in the house, Ms. Wax will kill me."

She gave Maggie a tug. Maggie barked again. Once. Twice. But she did not move.

"Okay," Eva decided. "We'll do it another way."

She bent to pick up the dog. She was

careful of Maggie's tummy. Her idea was to carry Maggie to the curb. At least the dog would have a chance to pee.

It was an awful idea. When the rain and wind hit the dog, she went nuts. She barked and snapped at Eva. Eva let her go. The leash slipped from her hands.

Maggie looked at her. For a moment, all was okay.

Then, it wasn't. The dog took off down the street at high speed.

Eva could not believe her eyes.

"Stop!" she called. "Maggie, come back. Where are you going?"

The dog stopped to look at her. Then she kept running.

"Get back here!"

Maggie didn't stop. She was a runaway dog.

9
MOMMA

Eva did the only thing she could think of. She took the other dogs up to the porch. Out of the rain. Then tied their leashes to it.

She ran after Maggie. She was lucky to see her about two hundred feet away. The rain pelted. The wind blew. The chase took her down many wet streets. Maggie ran into some trees. The ground was muddy. Eva sank into the mud.

You can't run in these things! →

Yuck! Why did I ever want to be a dog walker?

They came out of the trees. Maggie ran for five more minutes. Then she quit. Eva was amazed to see that they were back in front of Ms. Wax's house. The dog was panting. In fact, she was too tired to bark when Eva picked her up.

"Got you!" Eva cried. Only when Maggie was in her arms did she look to see if the other dogs were still on the porch. They were. Well, that was one good thing.

Eva brought Maggie to the porch. She tied her leash. She took off her rain gear. Then she went inside to find towels.

She wrung out her clothes. She wrung out her clothes. They were like soaked rags. Then she dried off the dogs. Only when they were dry did she call Carmen.

"Carmen? It's me. I need help."

"What's up? I think this is the first time you've called me in a year. You always text."

Eva NEVER calls. This must be serious!

"Total mess." Eva pushed some water off her face. "Look. Can you come and walk Swaps and the Great Dane? I have to stay with Maggie. She ran away from me. I just got her back."

"Whoa. In this rain? Anyway, no can do. My mom's taking me to the dentist."

"But it's urgent!" Eva looked at Swaps and the Great Dane. They had to get back to their owners.

Maggie looked at her. And moaned. Then she went to the front door and tried to push it open. Then she whined some more. It was a new kind of whining.

Oh no.

Eva had done her reading. She knew what was happening.

"Carmen? Listen to me. I think Maggie is about to have her pups. I need to take her inside. Call Paul … Yes. I know, I know. I hate him too. Ask him to come for these dogs. Then call Ms. Wax. Tell her to call me. Or come home. Or call me and then come home. And get over here right away. As soon as you can."

Maggie cried even louder. So did the other dogs. It was a group wail.

"You're sure?" Carmen asked.

"Sure I'm sure! Now let me get the dogs inside. Bye!"

Eva opened the door. Maggie ran inside. Eva unleashed the other dogs and put them in the basement. She gave them some food and water. After that, she went to check on Maggie.

This should keep them busy...

The white dog was on her bed. As Eva stared in wonder, her first pup started to come out. It was small, wet, and helpless.

Maggie was now a momma dog.

10
THE GIFT

By sunset, the rain was done. Inside the Wax house, there was a big crowd around Maggie. Eva and Carmen. Their parents. Grumpy Mr. Gold. Even Ms. Wax. She drove home as soon as Carmen called her.

A rare smile →

Everyone likes puppies! Even grumpy Mr. Gold.

Paul was there too. He had agreed to walk Swaps and the Great Dane. Then he asked to come over. He had never a seen dog give birth. Neither had Eva.

It was so cool. There were five pups so far. They were tiny. Smaller than Eva's hand. Ms. Wax told Eva how sorry she was. She was wrong about what day the puppies would come. "I should have been here the whole time," she kept saying.

The smallest puppy I've ever seen!

"Don't worry, Ms. Wax," Eva assured her. "It's fine. Maggie's doing great."

Maggie licked each pup as it came out.

Then she bit each cord. After that, she got each pup warm in the bedding.

"I think there's one more," Mr. Gold said.

He was right. Everyone watched as Maggie gave birth to one more. This one was very small. It did not breathe on its own.

"Is it going to die?" Eva asked.

"I don't think so. Watch," Mr. Gold told her.

Eva saw Maggie lick the pup's face. She went hard at the little nose. She pushed the pup with her paws. Finally, the puppy took a breath.

Please let this work...

61

"I think we should name that one Eva," Paul joked. "Because it just won't give up."

Even Eva laughed at that.

When the small pup was clean, and Maggie was happy, everyone cheered. Now the dog needed to rest.

Eva looked at Carmen. "Um, this has been fun. But we've got dogs to walk."

"You're on top of it for sure," Ms. Wax said. "You girls would be fine dog owners. How about if each of you take a puppy? Not tonight, of course. But when they're weaned. When they can eat on their own."

Oh. My. Gosh. Eva wanted a dog so much. So did Carmen. But their parents …

Our dogs could be best friends too!

Each girl turned to her mother.

Eva's mom grinned. "Well, I think you're ready. When I was your age, I got a dog."

"So did I," said Carmen's mom.

Both girls yelled with joy.

Eva was thrilled. There would be more dogs to walk. But it would not be too many dogs. And she would always walk her dog herself.